THE UNEXPECTED NANNY

A SINGLE DADDY-NANNY SHORT ROMANCE

MICHELLE LOVE

HOT AND STEAMY ROMANCE

CONTENTS

1. Chapter One	1
2. Chapter Two	6
3. Chapter Three	13
4. Chapter Four	20
5. Chapter Five	27
6. Chapter Six	33
7. Chapter Seven	39
8. Chapter Eight	43
9. Chapter Nine	49
10. Chapter Ten	51
About the Author	55

Made in "The United States" by:

Michelle Love

© Copyright 2021

ISBN: 978-1-64808-122-4

ALL RIGHTS RESERVED. No part of this publication may be reproduced or transmitted in any form whatsoever, electronic, or mechanical, including photocopying, recording, or by any informational storage or retrieval system without express written, dated and signed permission from the author

❦ Created with Vellum

CHAPTER ONE

Aiden

Laughter was all I could hear as my little three-year-old daughter, Joy, ran through the aisles of the children's toy store I'd taken her to for her birthday. With no idea what to buy her, I had decided to bring her, so she could pick out exactly what she wanted—not that she needed a damn thing. Her playroom was full of things. But birthdays merit presents, so there we were.

As a single father of a little girl, I often found myself wondering what Joy wanted. I sometimes erred on the side of too girly for her. She had a streak of tomboy in her, I could already see. She wasn't a thing like her mother had been.

Joy's mother, Tanya, my wife of four years, met with an early death that nearly cost me my daughter as well. The two had gone on a boat ride with one of Tanya's male friends—one whom I knew nothing about. Nor did I know they were going out on his sailboat that day. I found that out when a set of police officers visited my home, where I'd barricaded myself in my study to finish the novel I'd been working on.

It was they who told me they needed me to come with them to the hospital. My wife and daughter had been in a boating accident. The boat had capsized when a sudden storm came up. All they knew for certain was that the Coast Guard had been called, the people on the boat had been found, and two out of three of them were dead. One was hanging on by a thread after nearly drowning, but had been resuscitated by one of the Coast Guards. The officers apologized to me, as they knew nothing more than that.

They had located me after finding a small, zippered, plastic bag in my wife's pocket that had her identification, her cell phone, and a business card with my name and information on it. Also on that card was a picture of me holding our one year old as I had my arm wrapped around my wife, indicating who I was to the authorities.

To say my heart was in my throat the entire way to the hospital just cannot begin to describe how I was handling the news. I mostly felt numb. I was dizzy, sick to my stomach, and praying that, by some miracle, I would get to the hospital to find them both alive, instead of only one of them.

My prayers went unanswered that day. I was taken to the lowest floor of the hospital first. There, I found my wife when they pulled out a stainless-steel tray from a small door on a wall that was full of them. Her wedding ring was still on her finger. The helpful doctor pulled it off and placed it in my hand, as he said, "Can you identify the man who was found with them for us? He didn't have any identification on him. We don't know who to call about his death."

I didn't really want to see another dead person, but I suppose that little thing most of us have inside our brains that tells us to be helpful, no matter what our problems might be, had me saying, "Sure."

Leaving my blue-skinned wife with soaked, stringy brown

hair where she was, the doctor opened another little door, and out came a man I did recognize. "That's the guy who cuts our grass. Julio. His family lives on the south side of Miami. I think I have his card at home, in a drawer in the kitchen. I can call you with it when I get back home, I guess."

"Could you possibly have someone go find that?" one of the officers asked me. "It's pretty important to notify the family as soon as possible."

"I guess there's no one better to trust than a cop. If I give you the code to get in and tell you where to find the card, can you go take care of that? I mean, my daughter's here, somewhere. I may not leave here for a while." I realized then that I was too calm. *Way too calm!*

When the doctor handed me the plastic bag that had been in my wife's pocket, and I saw her cell inside of it, I placed my hand on one of the officer's arms. He looked at it, then at me. "You okay?"

"No," I said then, as it felt as if the floor was moving in waves under my feet. "Not at all."

I suppose they caught me when I passed out. I had never fainted in my life. And when I woke up to find the three men looking at me and the doctor shining a light in my eyes, I sobbed. I continued crying, even as they helped me to sit up on the cold floor of the morgue.

Even though I was beyond distraught, I had an idea the cops could find Julio's phone number on my wife's cell. "Take out her phone, and see if Julio's name is on her contact list."

One of the officers did as I'd said, and when he looked at the phone, I could see the truth written all over his face, as he said, "Yes, here's his personal cell and his home phone. And there's a text here. It's ... oh, nothing. Anyway, I have the number to his home. Let me make the call. Do you think you should be seen by a doctor, Mr. Cooper?"

"I don't know what I need. I believe it might help me to see my daughter." I was picked up and helped to the bathroom, where the very nice officers helped me wash my face and pull myself together a bit. Then they escorted me to the elevator. "You read something in her text messages about her and him, didn't you?"

"That's nothing you need to focus on right now, Mr. Cooper. You have a daughter to worry about. Focus only on that. For now, she's the only thing in this world that matters," one of the men said to me. And he was right.

It was two days later before I allowed myself to look at my wife's phone and her texts. She and Julio had been having sex for about a month, it seemed. He, too, was married, and I didn't feel it necessary to let that poor young woman know about the affair. Why hurt her?

She was naïve and never asked why my wife and kid were out with her husband on his boat. Either it never occurred to her that it wasn't something people did with the guy who cuts their grass, or she was one of those women who hide their head in the sand about their husband's infidelities. I just wished I could've been as naïve as she was.

Instead, I was driven to find out everything I could about what my wife had done. My daughter was recuperating in the hospital, and I found myself going through everything Tanya owned. Her laptop was the motherload of information. The lovers had exchanged emails.

There was even an email about divorcing me, taking half of everything I had worked so hard for, and running off with him, taking my baby with them. It was safe to say, if those two hadn't perished in a tragic accident, then I might've ended up in prison for murdering them both. So, like they say, some tragedies are meant to happen.

At least my daughter was going to live, and she and I could make our own happy family. *Fuck her cheating whore of a mother!*

In the two years that passed after Tanya's death, I made my daughter, Joy, my entire life. I'd written a few books that had done really well and which had given me a nice nest egg. So I could take an extended vacation to settle into my life as a single dad, to a daughter I adored.

But that nest egg was running low, and it was time for me to get back on the hamster wheel of writing. My work had given us a very nice lifestyle, and I wasn't about to lose it all because I hadn't gotten my shit completely together. My libido was zilch; my mind was blank; and my inspiration was nada.

Somehow, I had to make the magic in my head work again. I knew it was something I needed to do, but I had no idea how to do it. So, when my little girl started jumping up and down and screaming that she wanted a toy that was up too high for me to reach, I went looking for someone to help me get it down, and I found a surprise that would change our lives.

CHAPTER TWO

Skye

On a typical Wednesday, I worked the afternoon shift at Kid's Toy World, in my hometown of Miami, Florida. Just getting back from a fifteen-minute break that I'd spent on my laptop, turning in assignments for my online classes I was taking in hopes of one day becoming a nurse, I smoothed out my baby blue smock.

A mess of long, blonde spiral curls bounced around the adorably round, cherub face of a little girl as she barreled toward me. "I found a monkey!"

Her words had me a bit confused, so I asked, "A real one?"

The little girl stopped and laughed, holding her tummy as she did. "No, silly! A stuffed one! You're so funny!" She took my hand in her chubby small one and led me away with her as she went on and on. "I like monkeys. I want a real monkey, but Daddy won't let me have one until I'm big enough to take care of it my own self. And he says that monkeys can bite you, on account of the sharp teeth they have. So, my monkey might have to go to a monkey dentist and get its teeth pulled out. But I think that's too mean. Don't you think that's too mean, lady?"

The pause in her rambling gave me the chance to answer her. "I do think that's a bit mean."

"See, I knew it was. Daddy says it's not as mean because if that monkey bit me, he'd have to put it in the zoo. Anyway, a stuffed monkey will have to do for now, and I found me a great big one. Only I can't reach it, and even my very tall daddy can't reach it. So, he said we needed to get some help, and you look like the right person to help Daddy and me. And has anyone ever told you that you're very pretty, and you smell like cotton candy? You don't have any more of that stuff, do you? 'Cause I like cotton candy very much, and today is my birthday too, so I can have some if you have any left."

"Happy birthday," I said when she took a breath.

"Joy!" a deep voice called out. "What in the world made you think you could run off like that? I was worried sick. I nearly called the police!"

We stopped and turned around as the little girl batted her eyelashes at me. "Oops, I forgot to wait for Daddy. This is my daddy, nice lady."

"I can see that. You two look just alike," I said with a smile. "The same blonde curls hung around the tall, muscular man's face. His ocean blue eyes sparkled as he gave me a shy nod.

It was hard to believe he was looking so timid. He was an Adonis. They could've made a statue out of him, and women everywhere would flock to see it.

"I'm sorry for shouting at you, Joy. It's just that you shouldn't ever run off like that, baby." He came to us and scooped her up in his strong arms. I couldn't help but notice how his huge biceps bulged under his tight, teal-colored T-shirt. The way his daughter was refusing to let my hand go had me standing so close to the man that I could smell the coffee he must've had earlier. It mingled with a musky scent that was all him.

"Um, little girl, you can let go of my hand now," I said, as things felt more than a little awkward.

"No," she said simply. "Daddy, this nice lady will help us get my monkey."

"That's nice," he said, then gave his kid a kiss on the top of her head. "But you're making her feel uncomfortable. You need to let her hand go, pumpkin."

"But I like her," she said, and my heart melted a little.

"And I like you," I told her. "You can hold my hand if you want to. Come on, let's go get your bear."

"Monkey," she corrected me.

"Monkey, yeah—I meant that." I had to walk backward as she held my hand, and it felt a little like her dad and I were dancing as we went to the aisle the toy was on.

There was a ladder not too far from there, and I looked at it, then at the little girl's grip on my hand. I had no idea what to say to her. When I caught her father's eye, he saw my distress. "Joy, she has to go get the ladder. You have to let the nice lady's hand go."

When she released my hand, it felt emptier than it had ever felt. "Okay," Joy said, then smiled and whispered something in her father's ear as I walked away to get the ladder.

I heard her and her father snickering behind my back and felt my cheeks heat with embarrassment. I had no idea what they were talking about, but I was fairly sure it had to do with me. I was always body conscious. I was what some called well-endowed. I called myself fat.

My mousy brown hair was pulled into a high ponytail, and I had spilled a bit of chocolate milk on my smock. I didn't usually care what I looked like when I was at work. But that day, with that gorgeous guy there, I cared a lot!

When I pushed the ladder, which was on wheels, over to where the monkey was, I found the guy looking me over. "So, Skye, that's a cool name."

I was shocked he knew my name and asked, "How do you know my name?"

He and his daughter laughed liked hyenas as he pointed at my name tag. I felt like an idiot, and my blush went one shade deeper as I climbed up the ladder to retrieve the monkey. How would I recover from that?

When I pulled the toy off the shelf, I heard the guy say, "Hand him on down here, sweetie."

Sweetie?

"Here you go, honeybunch," I said with a smile, as I held out the stuffed animal to him. Then I saw his daughter, as he had her held up so she could reach some other toy.

When my eyes met hers, she went into another fit of giggles. "You called my dad honeybunch!"

I couldn't speak. I was utterly humiliated. Then he spoke. "I think she was talking to you, Joy."

"Yeah, I was," I said much too quickly, as I climbed down the ladder, still holding the giant monkey. "Here you go, Joy. Can I help you find anything else?

"Um, I think this is enough toys for me today. My daddy's takin' me to eat at my favorite place when we leave here. Do you like chicken nuggets?" Joy asked me.

"Are you kidding me? Who doesn't?" I said with a smile, then tousled her curls. "Your daddy's very good to you, isn't he?"

With a shrug, she said, "I dunno. I guess he is. I mean, I don't have nobody else to compare him to."

"Okay, Joy, let's get going. This nice lady has work to do," her father said, then took her hand as he carried her stuffed monkey. She carried the doll she'd picked out in her other hand and looked back at me as he tugged her to leave.

"Um, uh, I wanted to see if you could go to lunch with me," the little girl said.

"Joy, she's working," her father said, as he kept on going.

I stood there like an idiot, just watching them leave, feeling odd for reasons I couldn't grasp. The way the little girl kept looking at me with her big blue eyes was unnerving.

He took her around a corner, and I lost sight of them. Turning around to put the ladder back where I had gotten it, I saw a cell phone sitting on the edge of one of the shelves. It had to be the kid's dad's. Picking it up, I hurried after them.

I found them standing in a line. Some woman was trying to talk to the little girl, commenting on her gorgeous curls. But Joy was burying her face in her father's leg, as she held tightly to it. "I'm sorry," her father said. "She's very shy."

The kid I'd met was anything but shy!

As I made my way to the man, the lady remarked, "That's an enormous monkey. Where do you plan on putting him?"

Joy still ignored the woman, who I got the feeling was trying to get the kid's attention to get to her daddy. Her father said, "Don't be offended, Miss. She never talks to anyone. Well, except for the lady back there. That was the first time she's ever talked to anyone, other than her grandparents and me. It's crazy, really."

I stopped for a moment to let that sink in. *She liked me!*

Shaking my head to clear it, as it didn't matter at all if that kid liked me or not, I stepped forward and said, "Sir, I think you forgot your phone."

Joy's head turned my way, and a smile split her face. "Hey, did you decide to come eat lunch with us?" She jumped up and down as she came to me and actually held up her arms for me to pick her up. Which I did, without thinking about it at all.

Before I could say another word, my shift manager walked

passed me, saying, "Skye, you have to take your lunch now, or you won't get one. You have one hour."

"Okay," I said, then I was stuck as Joy had heard what he'd said.

"You can come to lunch with me. Lucky me! This is my best birthday ever!"

I caught the other woman's eye as she gave me the once over. "Her grandmother?" she asked, with a smirk.

Joy's father wasn't smiling as he said, "No, just someone Joy's decided to cling to. So, are you free to go to lunch with us, Skye?"

His blue eyes looked a bit sad. It was then that I noticed the wrinkles at the corners of them. There was one frown line that ran across his forehead. It was plain to see that he didn't want me to go, but for his kid, he'd do just about anything. *Even take a stranger on a birthday lunch!*

Joy took my face in her hands and said, "Pleaseeee..."

"How can I say no to that?" I said, then gave her father a nod. "Sure. I can follow you in my car."

"No, ride with me! Pleaseeee...." Joy pleaded with me.

"Please, ride with us," her dad said. "My name's Aiden Cooper, by the way. I don't expect you to get in a car with a complete stranger.

"*The* Aiden Cooper?" I asked in surprise. "How did I not recognize you? I've read everything you've ever written. I love horror stories, and you're like a master at them."

I was shocked to see his cheeks go a light shade of pink. "Thanks. I haven't written anything lately."

"I know. I've been wondering what happened to you," I said, then felt badly about it, as I dimly recalled a news story on him a couple of years back. His wife had died, and his daughter almost died. And there was some other news along with that. His wife was cheating on him, too, and he'd found that along with all the other bad news.

And all I could think was, *poor man*.

3

CHAPTER THREE

Aiden

My eyes kept migrating to the rearview mirror. Skye was sitting in the backseat with Joy, who was chattering away like a little bird. It wasn't like my daughter at all to be doing that with anyone but me. She wasn't even that comfortable with her grandparents.

I knew I shouldn't be looking at the woman who was kind enough to go to lunch with my kid. But I couldn't help but notice how her brown eyes had a ring of green around them, or how her face was naturally beautiful, even without any makeup on. Thick, dark lashes framed her soulful eyes. Her nose was turned up at the end, giving her a cute, slightly fairy-like look.

When Joy took a breath, I asked, "Do you have any kids, Skye?"

"Me?" she asked, with a very high voice. "I'm just twenty-two. I haven't even had a real relationship yet."

"Oh," I said, then felt stupid for asking.

"Plus, I have work and my online school. Kids are something that might come for me in the distant future," she added.

"What're you going to school for?" I asked, as I looked at her through the rearview mirror.

"I want to be a nurse," she said, and I found her smile sweet. "A pediatric nurse, to be more precise."

"Well, you're certainly a natural with kids. Let me tell you, Joy has never had this reaction to anyone before." I tapped the steering wheel as a notion flitted through my brain. I'd need someone to help me with Joy, so I could get back to writing. And the young lady in the backseat might be the one who could do that for me.

"I think you'll be a great nurse and mommy," Joy said as she played with a lock of Skye's chocolate colored hair. "Your hair's so pretty. I wish mine was like yours."

I watched as Skye twirled her finger around one of my daughter's blonde curls. "I love your hair, Joy. It's far more beautiful than mine is. You're one lucky girl, with this head of hair you have."

"Nah," Joy said. "Yours is much better."

"I think you both have gorgeous heads of hair," I said, earning myself a little blush from Skye, which I found utterly adorable.

We pulled into the place my daughter had picked for her birthday lunch. It wasn't where I'd have chosen to take her or Skye, but it wasn't my birthday.

"Yeah! Nuggets!" Joy squealed.

After parking, I found Skye helping Joy out of her car seat. "So many buckles," she said.

I got out of the car and opened the back door. "Let me do it. It's complicated." Our fingers touched as I reached in. I was a bit surprised to find sparks shooting through me. But I'd been celibate for over two years, so I should've expected it.

"Okay," Skye said, then got out of the car.

After getting Joy out, she and I made our way to Skye, who

was waiting at the door for us. Joy rushed up to her and held out her arms, wanting to be picked up again. This was something she didn't usually do, even with me.

Skye scooped her up with ease, and I opened the door for them, letting her walk in before me. "Thank you. What a gentleman you are, Mr. Cooper."

"I'm only thirty. Mr. Cooper is hardly what I should be called. Aiden would make me happier," I told her, as my hand moved instinctively to rest on the small of her back.

Joy's arms were wrapped around Skye's neck, and I had never seen my daughter so happy. "Nuggets for us both, Daddy."

"Maybe Skye would like something else, Joy. Let her tell Daddy what she wants," I said and watched Skye's cheeks blossom into a scarlet color. "Oh, poor choice of words. Anyway, Skye, what would you like?"

"Nuggets are cool," she said. "And a small soda. Any kind is fine with me."

"I can afford to splurge today," I told her, as I chuckled. "How about a large drink?"

"Sure, whatever. I'm easy," Skye said, then her cheeks went even redder. "I didn't mean ... oh, Lord. Anything is fine. Should I take Joy to the play area and get her shoes off, so she can play?"

"That would be sweet of you," I said. "Is that okay with you, Joy?"

"Yes, please take me to play. Oh, Daddy, fries too, and ketchup!"

"Got it," I said and watched them walk away.

When I turned back around, the little old lady who was waiting to take my order said, "What a beautiful family you have there. You must feel pretty lucky."

"Huh? Oh, she's not mine," I said, then stopped. What did I care what this lady thought? "Thanks. How about some nuggets, fries, and a hamburger, with three large drinks?"

"Sure, what kind of sauce would you like for the nuggets?" she asked me, leaving me wondering what kind of sauce Skye liked.

"Give me one of each," I said, then paid the bill and went to fill up the cups, while I waited for the food to come out.

Again, I was left wondering what type of soda Skye really liked. I settled on Mr. Pibb, because who doesn't like that?

After the order was placed on a tray, I took it, and the drinks, and went out to the play area to find my daughter and her new friend. Skye was sitting at a small, round table, with a clown face on it. "Go, Joy!" she shouted, as my daughter ran through the maze at the top of the structure.

"Wow, she's never ventured up that high before," I said, as I placed the food on the table, then ditched the tray on the table next to ours. "You have a remarkable effect on her."

I took the seat opposite hers and pushed the packets of sauce over to her. She turned around to face me. "Thanks. You're really a great dad. I wish I'd had one as good as you. Mine was always gone. I hardly ever saw him. It was just my mom and me most of the time. Until I turned fifteen, then it was just me."

"Your dad left?" I asked her, as I handed her a straw.

She took it and said, "No, he didn't leave my mother. She just started going out and staying out. Dad worked out of town. I guess they had an open marriage or something."

"Oh," I said, feeling like I'd dug too deep. "How committed are you to that job?" I wasn't sure why I was even asking her that question. Words seemed to be coming straight from my brain and right out of my mouth, with no forethought what-so-ever.

"It's a job. And it's pretty easy," she said. "I won't keep it once I get my nursing degree, if that's what you mean."

"I meant that I might have a job for you, if you're willing to let that one go." I still couldn't believe what I was saying. This was not like me at all. It was more like what a character in my head would say.

The thing was, I hadn't had any of the voices in my mind that I'd had when I was actively writing. When I was in my prime, before the incident, I talked to myself all the time. The characters in my head spoke to me and one another nearly continuously.

I had to admit to myself that my being so wrapped up in my stories and my writing might have been why Tanya went looking for love in all the wrong places. I knew I'd have to learn how to divide my attention between my writing and Joy. It'd be tough to learn how to do it, but I would do it for my little girl. The woman Joy had inadvertently found might just be my key to making it all work out.

"What kind of job are we talking about?" Skye asked, then popped a naked nugget into her mouth.

"No sauce at all for you?" I asked her.

She shook her head. "Nah. So about this job?"

"Oh, um, well," suddenly I was hesitating about offering her a babysitting job. I wanted it to sound more prestigious than that. "Have you ever considered being a nanny?"

"A nanny?" she asked, as she seemed to be thinking it over. "I can honestly tell you that I've never thought about doing that."

"Hey, look at me, Skye!" Joy called out, then jumped off the top of the platform, landing in the ball pit.

Skye jumped up and clapped, as she whooped and hollered, "Way to go, Joy! Great jump, kiddo!"

"Thanks," Joy said, as she made her way to the side, most likely to do it all over again.

My heart was pounding with how great the woman was with my kid. When she sat back down, and I saw pure and honest happiness radiating all over her, I just said it, "Be my nanny, Skye. Joy needs you."

"Huh?" she asked with a frown on her pretty face. "I honestly know nothing about kids. Really, Aiden. You need to hire a pro for something that important."

"Can you run some bath water that won't freeze or scald my kid?" I asked her.

"Well, yeah, I can make a decent bath. I can cook, too. I can do the normal things. But taking such an active role with anyone's child, well, that's daunting." She sipped her drink and smiled. "Hey, they had Mr. Pibb? It's my absolute favorite, but you hardly ever find it. Thanks, Aiden. You're a mind reader."

"That's how I feel you are with Joy. Please take the job. I can pay you seven-fifty a week. You'll have complete access to my second car, a Range Rover. And room and board. Plus, the job of nanny will look great on your resume when you go to get a job as a pediatric nurse. Don't you think?"

"Well, yeah, it would, I suppose. And seven-fifty? Do you mean seven dollars and fifty cents an hour?" she asked me, as she looked into my eyes.

"No, I mean seven hundred and fifty dollars a week. And you'll only have to take care of Joy from nine to five each weekday. You can have weekends off," I sweetened the deal, to see if I could get her to agree.

"When would this start?" she asked.

"ASAP. I'd love it if you could start today. I think that would be the ultimate present for Joy," I said, and then I saw a twinge of something in her eyes. A little worry, maybe.

"A present for her, huh? I don't know," she said, then popped another nugget into her mouth.

"Don't think in those terms. I just mean, it would be a great thing for her. Starting today would be great too. I could help you move your stuff into our home after you get off work. I know you'll probably want to give them two weeks' notice, but I'll make it worth your while if you quit today. How about a cash sign-on bonus?" I took a thousand dollars, all in hundreds, out of my wallet and placed them on the table in front of her.

"Damn! Have I keeled over or something? Am I actually on the way to the hospital in the back of an ambulance and not sitting at this table with a chunk of money in front of me?" She shook her head, as if she was unable to believe something like this could happen to her.

"It's real. Take the cash, and come be my daughter's nanny." I reached over and grasped her hand. "Pleaseee...."

After taking in a deep breath, she looked at me with a smile. "How can I say no to that? I'll do it! Oh, my God! I'll do it, Aiden!" Then she gave a little scream.

And just like that, I'd hired a nanny for my kid!

CHAPTER FOUR

Skye

I knew I should've told Aiden about my brief stint as a stripper when I was eighteen. But I was afraid he'd look at me as a bad influence on his little girl, so I kept that locked away. Only a few people knew about it, after all. And I doubted Aiden Cooper ever rubbed elbows with drug dealers and bar bouncers anyway.

So, I ended my career as a customer service rep at the toy store to become a big-time nanny to the ultra-wealthy horror writer's little princess. And things went well that first week.

We easily settled into a nice routine. His housekeeper made breakfast for us all, then she got to work, cleaning the house. Aiden went to his study to write, and I played with Joy. It was easy and fun.

His housekeeper only worked on the weekdays until noon, then she went to her home, wherever that was. She barely spoke English. That left me to make lunch, and Aiden would join Joy and I to eat the meal. Then he'd go back to writing, and I'd take Joy to her bedroom where I read to her until she fell asleep for her two-hour nap. Then I'd take a break and go into my bedroom, taking the baby monitor so I could hear her when she woke up. I'd get in some online school work, then make Joy a snack when she was done napping.

Aiden insisted on taking us out for dinner every night. We always went someplace nice, and Joy and I would get dressed. It was a nice way to spend my time. And things were going so well, I had no doubts that I'd made the right decision.

The first weekend came, and there I was, off of work. I wasn't supposed to do a thing for Joy. I was supposed to let Aiden take care of her all by himself. He'd always done that, so it wasn't like he couldn't handle it. It was me who was finding it hard to be doing nothing.

I had no idea what to do with myself that first day of freedom. So, I went for the old go-to and started doing school work. I was at the end of a section when a knock came at my door. "Skye, can I come in?" It was Aiden.

"Sure," I said, as I sat my laptop on the bed next to me. I had put on shorts and a V-neck T-shirt, since I'd be doing nothing all day.

"Are you busy?" he asked me, as he gestured to my open computer.

"Not anymore. What can I do for you?" I asked him, thinking he might need me to take Joy off his hands for a while.

"We're going to the beach. I wanted to know if you'd like to come with us?"

"Uh, well, you said you didn't want to lose what you and Joy had. You told me you wanted to spend time alone with her. Don't you think it'd be better if I didn't go?"

He chewed his lower lip, as he put his hands in the pockets of his baggy shorts. "Yeah, I know what I said. But, here's the thing. It's been a week, and I've yet to come up with an idea for a novel. And since you said you've read my work, I thought a nice outing might help me get inspired. And I could bounce ideas off you."

"Sure!" I said with enthusiasm. "I'd love to help you. Let me put on my bathing suit under these clothes, and I'll be ready to go."

"Great!" came his happy response. "See you downstairs when you're ready, then."

I went through the drawer that had my bathing suits in it and found that all I had were skimpy bikinis. I didn't think it would be appropriate to wear any one of them, but I had no choice. I picked out a black one and put it on, then pulled on some black shorts and a black spaghetti-strap shirt over the top. Slipping into my flip flops, I pulled my hair up into a ponytail and headed out for a day of being helpful to a famous author.

As I got to the front door, I found Aiden staring at me. It made me secretly happy to find him looking at me as a woman, rather than a nanny. "I'm ready."

"I can see that. Don't you have any sunglasses?" he asked me.

I shook my head. "No."

He pulled open a drawer on the Queen Anne desk that sat by the front door. When he pulled out a black box and took a pair of Ray Bans out, handing them to me, I shook my head again. "Yes, you can have these. I have several pairs. I'm not going to take no for an answer."

Reluctantly, I took the expensive glasses and found Joy pulling at my shorts. "Carry me, Skye. I want to hold you."

She'd come up with this cute way of getting me to pick her up or hold her on my lap. So, I fell for her charms again, taking her into my arms, as I followed Aiden out of the huge house.

Aiden acted modest about what he'd accumulated in his short time. A six-bedroom home that I thought of as a mansion, but that he told me wasn't nearly the size of an actual mansion. He just liked to call it his home. He had a swimming pool in the backyard that he'd yet to fill up, because Joy didn't know how to swim yet. It sat empty, with the gate locked. And there were three garages that I'd never been into, on top of the one that was attached to the house, where his BMW and the Range Rover he let me drive were parked.

I followed him across the paved drive to one of the garages. He hit a button on the side of one of the three doors that ran along the front of it, and, when it moved up, I saw a shiny red, four-door Jeep. "Nice," I said.

"Yeah, Daddy likes to drive this when we go to the beach," Joy said.

I saw there was already a car seat in the back of the passenger seat and put her into it. I strapped her all in, then went to get in behind Aiden. "Hey, how about you sit up front? I don't want to feel like you guys' chauffeur."

"Are you going to be okay back here, all alone?" I asked Joy.

"Sure," she said, as she kicked her little, white sandaled feet and smiled like crazy. Her tiny sunglasses were perched on her nose, and she pushed them up. "Come on! Let's go!"

I hurried to get in the front seat and found Aiden smiling at me. "Buckle up. I like to go fast."

"Oh, my goodness," I said, as I did as he told me to. The wind whipped around us as he took off.

As we went down the road, Aiden pointed out an old lighthouse. His hand was in front of my face, as he said, "I've been in that one. It's kind of creepy. You think you might want to go in there with me sometime?"

"Okay," I said and found him resting his hand on my thigh. I glanced at it, but didn't say a thing. I liked the way it felt lying there. The way his rugged hand looked on my creamy thigh was pretty attractive to me.

The truth was, I'd looked at Aiden a lot in that week. He was handsome, sweet, kind, and funny. I knew he had a sense of humor, as his books always had a thread of humor in them.

It was nice to see that he was relaxed with me. I felt relaxed with him, too. But I wasn't about to touch him, even if he felt like touching me. I was still his employee in my mind.

He moved his hand after a while, when he had to make a sharp turn that called for two hands on the steering wheel. His hand didn't come back to rest on my leg after that, and I was sorry about that.

When we got to the beach and things had settled down, as Joy played in the sand with her toys, Aiden and I sat back on chairs he'd had in his Jeep. "I'm thinking about something with a little romance in it," he said, completely out of the blue.

"Huh?" I asked him.

"My next book. I think it should have some romance in it. I read this one novel. It was called a dark romance. I liked it. But, to be honest, I'm not much on romance. I never have been."

"Then maybe you should stick to what you know," I said as I peered at him over my sunglasses.

"I've changed, Skye. I'm not that man anymore, so I'm not that writer anymore. And I want romance." His eyes penetrated mine as he spoke.

"Maybe I can help you find a girlfriend, Aiden," I said as I had no idea what else to say. "Maybe one of those online …"

"No!" he nearly shouted. "No, nothing like that." He looked at Joy, and I did too. She was singing away to herself, oblivious to either of us. I shivered when he reached over and placed his hand on my thigh again. "I don't want Joy aware of this at all. If things don't work out, then I don't want her to be hurt."

"What are you talking about?" I asked, as I was utterly confused.

"What would you think about messing around with me?" he

asked, the same way someone would ask you if you wanted to share their popcorn.

"You don't have a romantic bone in your body, do you, Aiden?"

"Maybe you could teach me. In private. At night, after Joy's fast asleep. Maybe you could sneak into my bedroom every now and then. Like a little seductress, thieving a little sex. What do you think about that?"

I was speechless. *What did I think about that?*

Not even I knew the answer to that. But I'd developed a secret crush on him from the first day. Each night, I had to masturbate before I could fall asleep. Knowing the man was only a couple of doors away, lying in his massive bed, most likely doing the same damn thing, had me turned on.

But this was real, not imagined. I was looking into his glistening eyes as he looked at me over his sunglasses. He gave me a wink, and I giggled. "Aiden, you're screwing around with me!"

"Not yet, I'm not. But I want to. Secretly, though. Joy can't know about this."

The rush of this being a big secret was making heat surge through my body and pool between my thighs. Could I do it? Could I bring myself to sneak into the man's bedroom and slink into his bed? Could I act like a naughty vixen?

"I'm a virgin, Aiden." It popped out of my mouth before I could stop it.

"Fuck me," he whispered. "Seriously?"

I could only nod. "But I'd like to do what you're saying. I just wanted you to know that part."

Movement in his lap had me looking down to find his cock was rising in his shorts. Straight up it went, as he stared at me. "I would be your first? You're not shittin' me, Skye?"

"I am not, Aiden."

He had to grab a towel to cover his erection. "Being a virgin, do you think you could actually bring yourself to come into my room?"

"I've thought about doing that a lot this last week. Why not actually do it? If you want," I said then bit my lower lip. *What the hell was I doing?*

His chest was rising and falling, and he seemed like he might be about to burst. "I want. I want it worse than I've ever wanted anything. Do you think you could take off your shirt and shorts and let me have a peek at what'll be coming to my bed tonight?"

"I could use a bit of cooling off. Maybe a dip in the water is in order, Aiden." I got up and took my shirt off first, then wiggled my bikini top to wrangle in my mountainous tits. *I swear he was drooling!*

When I dropped my shorts, he leaned forward and pressed his hand on my stomach. "When you come to me tonight, wear only a robe and take it off when you get to my bed. I have to see this without a stitch covering you. You're built like a brick house, baby. Now, go play in the water."

For the first time in my life, I felt sexy. It was the way he looked at me that left me with no inhibitions. I could see it all in his eyes. He liked my body, and he liked it very much.

As I walked away, Joy saw me going and jumped up to come along. I felt a little bad about what I was doing, or going to do, with her daddy, but dads need love too.

CHAPTER FIVE

Aiden

I couldn't believe I'd said it to Skye, finally. I had dreamed about her every night since she first slept under my roof. She was one voluptuous, young beauty. When she told me she was a virgin, I nearly exploded. It was all I could do to hold myself back.

And now it was nighttime in my home, where I was expecting my dreams to come true. I'd showered, shaved, and spritzed my body with some great smelling cologne—a thing I didn't often do. As a matter of fact, I hadn't used any cologne in well over two years.

When nine o'clock turned into ten o'clock, I began to get worried. I had Joy asleep at eight-thirty, and Skye knew that. Had she decided not to do what I so desperately wanted?

I turned the light off and settled into the bed to try to go to sleep. There'd be no use staying awake and feeling the terrible sense of frustration. When my unlocked door cracked open a smidgeon, I sat up. "Skye?"

"Shh," she hissed.

I laid back on the pillows and watched her silhouette enter my bedroom for the very first time. She closed and locked the door behind her, then came toward me, dropping the robe as she did and showing me her incredible curves. I wanted more light. I reached out and turned on the lamp beside my bed.

Sucking in my breath, I gazed at her body. Creamy smooth skin glowed in the dimly lit shadows. Her hair was down and hanging over her shoulders. Her eyes were dark and haunting. "I need you to make me a woman." She stopped and looked down.

My cock went rock hard in record speed. "Come to me, baby." My voice was a husky whisper.

I pulled the blanket back, revealing my lack of clothing, as well as my erection. When she looked at me, then at my cock, she gasped. "Oh, shit! I had no idea. Oh, God, Aiden!"

"I know, I'm kind of hung, baby. I'll be gentle. I promise." I reached out for her hand and pulled her to me. "Do you trust me to take this gift you're giving me, Skye?"

I could see she was nervous, but she was also intensely aroused. "I trust you."

Pulling her to sit on the bed, I cupped the back of her neck and pressed my lips to hers the way I had wanted to that very first day. The kiss was every bit as sweet as I thought it'd be. Our tongues slowly caressed the other's as our hands moved over the other's back.

Hers felt like satin on my skin as they flowed over it. It had been so damn long since I'd felt a woman's touch, and never had Tanya's, or anyone else's for that matter, stirred something so deep inside me.

I don't know if it was because of the week-long nightly masturbation sessions where I envisioned Skye in my bed, or what, but the woman felt amazing in my arms.

Our mouths parted, and I kissed a sweet trail along the

length of her long, elegant neck. Skye moaned as I did and pressed her body to mine. Her breasts mashed against my chest, and I could feel the fast pace of her heartbeat. "Don't be afraid."

"I wish I wasn't," she said. "But I am. Help me stop thinking, Aiden."

With that, I pulled her to lie down and moved my body over hers. I'd be easy with her and show her how she could find so much pleasure in this. "Has anyone ever made you orgasm, other than yourself?"

When she shook her head, I had to smile. "So, your first not personally-stimulated orgasm will belong to me then?"

"Yes," she said, as she looked at me. She moved her hand over my cheek. "Aiden, I want you to know that I'm on the pill. I started taking it when I was sixteen, to regulate my periods."

"Good to know. It's been so damn long since I did this that I totally forgot about birth control." I moved my hands to her ample tits and tugged at her nipples. They hardened with my touch.

Taking one of them in my mouth and giving it a gentle suck, I licked the tip and had her hands tangling up in my hair as she purred. She was so into it, in a way my wife had never been. Her chest rose and fell with breaths that were getting faster.

I slowed my attention to her delicious breast, in order to give her a real treat. "Baby, I'm going to eat you out."

"Oh, God," she moaned, as I kept my eyes on hers and trailed my tongue down her stomach. A small patch of dark hair hid her jewels from me. I parted it and found her pearl already swollen with desire.

"Mine are the first lips to ever touch this place on you?" I asked her.

"Yes," she moaned as she grabbed each side of the pillow she was resting her head on. "Yours are the first."

I secretly hoped they'd be the last, but I wasn't about to go to that place just yet. This was our first time, and I had no idea if things would work out for us. I wasn't about to tell her that I was making her mine. But I didn't want her letting anyone else do this to her. I was kind of torn.

But my brain called the shots, and out of my mouth came, "This is mine, do you understand me? As long as we're doing this, I want no other person to have you. Tell me you understand me, Skye."

"You want it secret and exclusive?" she asked me, with a perplexed expression.

"Yes," was my simple answer.

"And what about you? Are you going to remain untouched by anyone else too?"

"I've remained untouched by anyone else for over two years. So, yeah, it goes for me too."

"Okay, then," she said and smiled. "Only you, Aiden."

A surge of power went through me with her words. She was all mine. No one else could have her. She was giving me everything. Her virginity, her first real orgasm, and she was giving herself to me and me alone. *I was on fire for this woman!*

I watched her as I kissed her intimate regions, and she bucked up to me with the first touch of my lips. "God!"

"Slow down, baby. It hasn't even gotten good yet," I said with a chuckle, then blew on her clit.

"Damn it," she groaned. "That's so amazingly wonderful."

"If you knew how I pounded myself while fantasizing about eating your pussy, you'd probably freak out." I licked her clit, making her moan even more.

She was going to get loud, I was sure, and I was happy to know that. Tanya was quiet, to the point that I didn't know what she liked and what she hated. She was just silent until it was over, then she'd say, "Thanks, babe" and push me to get off her.

Skye was an active participant, which I found I liked very much. Her moans tripled when I pushed one finger into her. She was tighter than I knew was possible. I pumped my finger in an attempt to spread her somewhat, before I tried to get my fat cock into her.

Over and over, I thrust into her as I licked her clit like an animal. Her cries of pleasure filled my ears as she soaked my finger with her juices. I had to taste her juices, so I pulled my finger out and stuck my tongue in, tongue fucking her as she came all over me.

Her breathing was harsh as she undulated. I gripped her ass to hold her still, so I could feast on the most delicious thing I'd ever tasted. I couldn't stop myself. It was her cries for me to fill her with my cock that drew my attention.

I pulled my mouth off her, reluctantly, as she said, "I want to feel you inside of me, Aiden. Please."

The time had come. I was about to pop my very first cherry. My dick was engorged with how much I wanted her. I found myself apologizing. "I'm sorry my cock's so big, baby."

Her laugh was cute and touching as she took my face in her hands. "Kiss me, Aiden. I want to taste myself on your tongue."

"Fuck, you're so hot, Skye!" I kissed her hard, moving my tongue all over her mouth.

Our kiss went on as she spread her legs wide for me. I settled into position, then placed the tip of my cock to her opening. It wasn't going in easily. Trying to take her attention away from what I knew would be painful, I kissed her more ravenously, easing my dick into her in tiny increments, until it was all in.

Pulling back to look at her, I saw one tear roll down her cheek. "I know it hurts ..."

She stopped me with her finger to my lip. "Shh, no it's not that, Aiden. It does hurt a little. It's just that this is so damn fantastic. That's what the tears are for. I've dreamed of this, and it's even better than anything I've ever thought it'd be."

As I stayed still, letting her small, young body get accustomed to mine, I saw it in her eyes. She had real feelings for me. But how could she have them so damn soon? This was just sex. We weren't falling in love. *Were we?*

CHAPTER SIX

Skye

I held his biceps, the way I'd wanted to since I first saw them that day at the toy store. They were tight, just the way I knew they'd be. His stomach was a masterpiece of chiseled abs, and his pecs were firm. I suppose the long bout of celibacy had him working out pretty intensely after Joy was put into bed each night.

Aiden was intense with me that first night. His body fit mine like a glove. Or was it that mine fit his that way?

It was hard for me to know where I ended and he began. We moved in a rhythm that felt like waves on the ocean. He was easy to be with, in a sexual way too. I felt relaxed and free with him. Just like the way he made me feel all the time.

We looked into each other's eyes as we had sex. I watched his go from stormy, to kind, to lust-filled once he decided he wanted to make me scream with desire for him.

My insides were on fire and quivering. Then my entire body began to shake, as he kept up a furious pace. When the explosions went off, I couldn't believe it.

Before I'd gone to his bedroom, I'd been reading in my room about having sex for the first time. Most of the articles I read online said not to expect to have an orgasm for a while. But here I was, bursting for the man. "Aiden!"

"Skye!" he groaned, then his body went limp.

We'd actually climaxed together. Our very first time, and we'd managed to get that far. Sex with Aiden was going to be great. I knew it was. I was on the verge of tears again, for reasons I didn't understand.

He'd dropped his head on my chest, then he kissed his way over it and up my neck. His lips landed on my ear. "I love you, Skye."

My entire body went tense. *Was this part of the act he wanted?*

I was to be a sexual thief in the night. It was a little secret act we were doing. An erotic play of sorts. And here he was, saying that he loved me. So, I decided it was part of the act and played along with him.

Running my hands through his curls, I whispered, "I love you too, Aiden."

I was rewarded with another round of kisses down my neck, then he made his way to my lips, where he kissed me softly, as he cupped my face in his large hands.

His cock began to pulse back to life, unbelievably. He began to make small strokes, and then we were going at it again. I wasn't even aware a man could get hard again that quickly.

Our bodies were covered in sweat. All I could hear was the sound of flesh slapping against flesh and ragged breathing from us both. His cock was so big, it hit a place so deep inside of me that it sent off shock waves with each hard thrust. It was all so intense, and I felt every part of my body, as we fucked liked I had only seen in movies.

"Wrap your legs around me," he said, and I hurried to do it. Then he got off the bed, with me wrapped around him.

My breath was knocked out of my lungs when he pushed me against the wall, gripping my ass in his hands. He moved me up and down his cock, as he banged it into me, hard and furiously.

My nails dug into his shoulders, as he used my body the way he needed to. I was elated to let him have me. And, this time, when we came together again, he was so different. Instead of the sweetness, he was rough, as he took a chunk of my hair and yanked it back.

His teeth raked over my neck, as he said with a harsh voice, "You like when I fuck you, baby?"

"Yes," I moaned.

"Yes, Master," he corrected me.

"Yes, Master," I cooed, as I played along with the new act he was going for.

When he gave my ass a sound slap, I whimpered. Then I found him taking me back to the bed. He sat down, and I was still straddling him. His smile was on the evil side as he picked me up, sliding my body off his dick that was still so long and thick. *He was definitely hung!*

"I'd like to spank you until you cry, Skye."

"Um, uh," I had no idea what to say.

"It's been a fantasy of mine," he said. "I've never done such a thing."

I hadn't been spanked since I was twelve and had snatched a pack of my mother's cigarettes. She'd paddled my ass good. And now Aiden wanted to do that too.

"Until I cry?" I asked him.

He nodded. "Then I want to kiss your ass and make it all feel better."

His horror novels came rushing to my mind. He'd never had sexual darkness in them, but I could see where his mind was going with this. How could he write dark romance without any real idea of how it felt?

I could be what he needed me to be. I knew I could. It was just an act. Sure, the physical aspects were real, but everything we were doing were merely acts. So, I bit my lip, then said, "I've been a very bad girl, Daddy. I'm sorry."

He smiled and said, "You lay over Daddy's lap, and let him show you what happens to little girls who don't do as they're told."

Not one to have ever thought a lot about erotic things like role playing, I was surprised to find my stomach was feeling tight. I wanted to feel his hand as he spanked my ass. I did as he'd told me to, laid my body over his lap, and closed my eyes as my pussy went wet, and I anticipated the first strike.

With a swift smack, he said, "Count them out loud, Skye."

"One," I said, finding that that hit hadn't really hurt. He gave me another, and it stung a little. "Two." The third one was right in the same place the other two had been, and it was beginning to really sting. "Three." But I was also feeling something inside of my body, too. I was feeling hot and sexy. When his palm landed hard on my ass again, tears suddenly sprang up. My voice cracked when I said, "Four." But I wanted more. I couldn't explain why I wanted more, but I did. I wanted him to keep doing it, until I was crying hard. His hand came down again. "Five," I croaked out.

"That's enough," he said.

"One more," I cried.

"Fuck, you're fucking amazing, baby."

"I was bad, Daddy. One more."

"Shit!" he hissed. Then he gave me one more really hard one, and a sob burst out of me.

He pulled me up as he stood, wrapping me in his arms, hugging me tight, and shushing me. "Shh, baby. It's all right. Daddy's not mad at you. You just had to learn, that's all. Let Daddy fix you."

Aiden laid me down on the bed on my stomach, as I continued to cry. But the crying was releasing something inside me. I could tell it was. It was therapeutic, it seemed.

Soft touches moved over my throbbing ass. I felt the wetness of his mouth as he kissed me there. He parted my ass cheeks and ran his tongue over my asshole. It was something I didn't know I liked. My crying started to ease up, as his tongue darted in and out of my asshole, then his fingers moved around to massage my clit.

Another orgasm was fast approaching, but he stopped before I could cum. Lifting me up, he pulled me back to my knees. My ass was up in the air, and he forced his hard cock into me with a swiftness that left me squealing from the pain it caused my now very sensitive tissues. "Aiden!"

"Shh," he said. "Head down."

I put my head on the bed, leaving my ass in the air. His strokes started slow and steady, as he ran his hands over my sore ass. Every part of me was sore, then. I had no idea how the morning would find me. *Incapacitated, probably!*

When he started raking his nails across my back and pounding me harder, he also added in, "You cum when I fucking tell you to, or I'll spank that ass again. You get me, baby?"

"Yes, Master," I answered him, through gritted teeth. I was shocked at how turned on I was.

Though it seemed impossible, my body went white hot as he went on and on. I was dying to release my orgasm, but my ass was begging me not to, as it still pulsed from the spanking. I cried when he finally shouted, "Cum!"

Tears flowed as my body came completely undone. I was shaking like a leaf. I could literally take no more. He fell on the bed next to me, spent as well.

With it all over, I waited until I had caught my breath, then I said in a soft voice, "And with that, I'll leave you alone, Aiden.

This was all a dream. Nothing really happened here. All a dream. A magical dream. And you never know when you'll have another one."

I eased my pained body off his bed and heard his light snores as I left the room, locking the door behind me. I didn't want Joy to accidentally stumble into his bedroom for some reason and find him in the state he was in.

After a hot shower, I pulled on a nightie and slipped into my bed. I'd taken the baby monitor and put it on my nightstand, so I could take any nighttime calls from Joy. *Her daddy needed his rest after all.*

7

CHAPTER SEVEN

Aiden

I woke up with a smile on my face, knowing I should've felt guilty about what I'd done to Skye. *She was a virgin for God's sake!*

But I couldn't feel that way. No matter how hard I tried, I just couldn't feel like it had been a mistake. *That was hands down the best sex I'd ever had!*

When I got up, I could barely walk. I hurt all over. The hot shower eased up the stiffness in muscles that had gone unused for far too long. And I was pretty set on continuing to work those particular muscles on a nightly basis. As long as Skye was still into it, that was.

I had no idea if she'd be up for it anymore. But I'd had enough to get me going. The book ideas were flooding my mind as I showered that Sunday morning. Steamy sirens were the heroines in every one of them.

Skye had no idea what she'd done for me, and I wasn't about to leave her unrewarded for it. When I dressed and left my room, I found Joy had already gotten up, as she wasn't in her room. I went to Skye's room and knocked, then opened the door. So what if I caught her naked?

But no one was in there, either. I went downstairs, heard them talking in the kitchen, and smelled bacon cooking. My dick went hard for the woman again. After a terrific night of sex, she got up with my kid on her day off, mind you, and she was making bacon. She was a winner in my book.

"Good morning, baby," I said, as I entered the kitchen and leveled my eyes on Skye. She gave me a smile that melted my underwear.

"Good morning, Daddy," Joy answered me.

Then I felt a little odd about my greeting. I was talking to Skye, after all. "How was your night, pumpkin?" I asked Joy, as I changed my demeanor into the fatherly style, rather than the dude who'd hit that style.

Out of the corner of my eye, I saw Skye start to bring that delicious smelling bacon to the table and couldn't help the smile that formed as I saw her stop and stretch just a bit before she continued. *Oh yeah, I had her where she could barely walk!*

Joy's high pitched voice took my attention as she said, "My night was all right, Daddy. But Skye fell off her bed, and her hips hurt today."

A laugh flew out of me, making my daughter give me a terrible look. "Oh, that's not funny at all. Daddy should talk to your nanny about how badly she's hurt, huh?"

"Yes, you should!" Joy chastised me. "She can barely walk. You shoulda seen her comin' down the stairs."

With Joy's approval, I turned my attention to the one female in the room I wanted to gather up in my arms and cuddle with. I turned to find Skye with her eyes cast down.

"Here you go, Joy. Here's the bacon and eggs I promised you. The toast is almost out of the toaster, honey bear."

Once she'd placed the plate on the table in front of Joy, and my daughter took her fork and plowed into it, ignoring us, I took Skye's hand and pulled her off to the pantry. "We should go over what groceries we need to buy. Do you mind helping me, Skye?"

"Sure, I can help," she said, as she looked over her shoulder at Joy.

I barely got her into the huge pantry and the door shut behind us before I pulled her into my arms and planted a much-needed good morning kiss on her sweet lips. "I'm sorry you're so sore, baby."

"I'll be okay. It comes with the territory," she said with a light laugh.

My eyes held hers for one moment too long. I could see she felt a little uncomfortable. "Seriously, are you okay? I mean, mentally. I went a bit further than I ever meant to."

Her hand felt so good as she moved it up my arm and rested it on my cheek. "I'm more than okay, Aiden. But I'll need a few days to recuperate from last night. I don't want you to get worried it won't happen again. I'm just really sore."

"You know, just because you're sore doesn't mean my naughty little nanny shouldn't visit her master, Skye. I can work out some of those tight muscles for you. I can treat you like a princess, too. A hot bath, in my deep jetted tub. Me holding you, washing you, rubbing your aching muscles." I had to stop talking and imagining that. I was getting a woody.

Her dark eyes looked into mine with such worry, I hated to see it. "Your naughty little nanny?" she asked with a frown. "Aiden, I don't know about this."

Oh, God no!

"Listen, give this a month, and if we still find ourselves enjoying one another, then we can let this secret out. I swear it to you. Please, don't stop, Skye." My heart was pumping harder than it had last night. And that was amazing!

"Aiden, my self-esteem may be too low to do this. I think we should ..."

That was all I allowed her to say. I kissed her hard, to remind her of what we shared, then I pulled away, quickly. "Just be quiet. Don't say a word. Don't ruin it. I've finally had a breakthrough. Please, don't spoil it for me."

With a curt nod, she said, "I won't spoil it, then. I'll be in your room tonight, if you need me."

I looked at her, then sighed, "Baby, I need you like I need air to breathe. You have no idea."

The look she gave me had me worried. It was one of those looks that asked, *are you for real?*

I didn't know if I was for real or not. All I knew at that time was that, if she told me to jump, then I'd say how high. She already had me that wrapped around her little finger. When her lips parted, I found even more of a reason to keep her.

"Aiden, since we're learning from each other, here, I'd like to ask you if I can perform my first oral sex act on you tonight. I'm going to research how to give a great blowjob. Would that be okay to try?"

"Oh, fuck me, Skye! You're unbelievable!"

"So, is that a yes?" she asked, as if she needed to.

"Yes." I kissed her again. "A million times, yes!"

CHAPTER EIGHT

Skye

With only three days to go until we met our one month anniversary and the date of coming out of the closet with what was now something we both considered to be a relationship, I found myself lying face down on my bed after a long night of wild sex.

To be able to stay in Aiden's bed and wake up next to him was a thing I was dreaming about. To hold his hand while we watched cartoons with Joy was like a fantasy to me.

We'd steal a kiss here and there. Cop a feel when Joy's attention was elsewhere. But other than that, it was just the nights when we could be real with one another.

I understood his concerns about his daughter. Hell, I had the same concerns. He'd confided in me about how he'd been in his marriage to Joy's mother. He closed himself off. Shut out her and their baby so he could devote his full attention to writing. And he was a spectacular writer.

Aiden Cooper hit The New York Times best seller list not once but three times before his wife died. I knew he could do it again. And with my help he was telling me that he was better than he'd ever been.

I wanted a peek at the manuscript he'd work on ten hours each weekday. Weekends he devoted himself to us. I was always included in his plans with Joy.

Aiden told me I'd made a remarkable change in his daughter. Her shyness with others had virtually disappeared. She was playing with other kids when we took her to the playground, a thing he said she'd never done before.

He even filled the swimming pool up and was letting me teach her how to swim. She hadn't got past the stage where she was wearing floaties, but she was making rapid progress. Joy loved showing her daddy how much she'd learned each day when he was through with his work. Things were going better than I expected.

A tap at my bedroom door had me rolling over, rubbing my tired eyes and saying, "Who is it?"

"Aiden. Can I come in?"

"Of course," I said then sat up in my bed, smoothing out my disheveled hair.

There was something wrong. I could tell it right away. His eyes were drooping at the corners. His mouth was turned down in a frown. And his hands were shaking.

"Joy, my brother called me early this morning." He stopped and looked at me with pain in his eyes. "I told him about you and me. And he was ..." He just stopped talking as he fidgeted.

"Aiden, just spit it out."

"He reminded me that I'm not as anonymous as most people. The fact is when I put out this new book then I'll be going on book tours and doing talk shows. And if I'm asked about who you are, and I tell them about you being my kid's nanny then how will that look? And the worst part is that Joy will know what I've done too."

"We're three damn days away from coming out with this. You and I will be legit before the book comes out. I don't' see a problem." I was shaking with fear that he was about to tell me we were over.

"Look, I know you might not understand. I don't really understand it all myself. But my brother pointed out that people will ask how we got together and what am I supposed to say when I'm asked that?" He looked confused and genuinely upset, but I was getting pissed.

"Who the fuck cares what you fucking tell them? We met in a toy store where I worked. No one needs to know any more than that. Christ, Aiden! Just tell me it's over already!"

"No, that's not what I want. Can't we just keep things as they are?"

My heart stopped. I quit breathing. "No."

Taking my face in his hands, he kissed my lips with a light kiss. "Please."

"No, Aiden. We come out with this, or we stop it." I was adamant. The hiding was fun at first, but it was getting old and quickly.

"You can't stop it any more than I can, Skye. Be honest with yourself," he said as he stroked my cheek with his fingertips.

"Me? I am being honest with myself. Why don't you try doing that? I know it's all still an act to you now. I thought we were getting past the sex act and into the real stuff. I was wrong. You want to play like we're a couple at night after your daughter goes to sleep. But you don't want it to be real. You're still closing yourself off."

"I am not!" he said with sudden indignation. "I've given more of myself to you than I've ever given anyone."

"Wrong," I said as I shook my head. "You gave Tanya your last name. You gave her the honor of being married to you. I've been better to you than she ever was. At least that's what you've told me. And for that, I get diddly squat? No thank you."

"How will Joy react to us suddenly being a real couple. Kissing and touching? Think about it. She'll be so confused," he said then got up and began pacing as he threw his hands up in the air. "You want me to put my kid in that kind of an emotional bind? That's pretty fucking selfish of you, Skye. I didn't think you were that kind of woman. The kind who'd put your feelings above an innocent child's."

"You cannot make me feel guilty over wanting to be your real girlfriend. Joy will accept things. Kids are more adaptable than grownups are. Just look at all I've done with her. You had her shy, and I easily got her out of that bubble. She'll be happy that we're happy and she finally has a real family."

When his eyes went narrow, and he glared at me, I felt the chill go straight to my heart as he said, "You're not her mother."

I narrowed mine right back at him as I reminded him of something, "And neither are you. She has no mother. And I'm the next best thing. Do you ever think about how growing up with no mom will affect her?"

"She has you as a nanny. That should be enough. And she has a father who's better than most." He turned around and walked toward the door. "I want things to keep going the way they are. So, this is settled. Come to my room anytime you want. But keep our private affairs private." And with that, he left my bedroom and me the maddest I'd ever been.

With it being Sunday and my day off, I hurried to shower and get dressed then hauled ass out of that house. I was set on not coming back until late that night.

"Skye!" I heard him calling out to me as I opened the door between the kitchen and the garage. "Where're you going?"

"Away!" I said then got into the Range Rover.

He got to the car door before I could close it. Grabbing it, he held it. "Are you quitting?"

"Not as Joy's nanny, I'm not. I'd never leave her. You, though. Yes, I'm quitting you. You see, I have a little secret I haven't told you. When I was eighteen, I was a stripper for three months. My mother and father went AWOL on me, and I had to pay the rent to keep the roof over my head. I had no idea how to get money quick, and I found myself walking down the street to a strip club."

"A virgin stripper," he said with a laugh. "Do you really expect me to buy that load of horse shit?"

"Buy it or don't. I don't give a flying rat's ass. Anyway, I danced and took my clothes off for money. I wasn't like the other strippers who got drunk or high. I did it all completely sober. And it sank in that I was degrading myself. Money or no money, I was using my body in a way that wasn't healthy. And I made myself a promise that I'd never do that to myself again."

"What does that have to do with me?" he asked as he looked as if he saw no parallels.

"I'll let you figure that out, Aiden. You're a smart man. Think on it for a bit. I'll be back late tonight. Like I said, I'll never quit on Joy. I love her like she was my own. And there's really nothing you can do to change how I feel about her. But you've certainly changed how I feel about you. I love you, Aiden. We both say it every night, and I know it's meant to be an act. But I love you for real. And I was a fool, but I thought you loved me too. Now let the fucking door go so I can leave."

He batted his big blue eyes at me as he said, "I don't want you to go. I feel like things will be different if I let you go, Skye. I don't want things to be different. I just want things to stay the way we have them, that's all."

"Well, I want more. Now, let me go."

He stayed put for a moment then he let the car door go and whispered, "I do love you, Skye. That's not a lie."

"Then prove it," I said and turned the car on, closed the door and pulled out of the garage as he watched me go but didn't want to say the words that would stop me.

CHAPTER NINE

Aiden

That day had been the longest one in my life. I called Skye three times, and she answered every time. She'd ask if Joy was alright to which I'd tell her she was and that I wanted her to come home. She'd ask if I'd changed my mind to which I'd tell her I hadn't but that I wanted her home.

Skye didn't come back until very late that night. At four in the morning, I found her coming in from the garage. I'd been sitting up, unable to sleep. "Hey," I said as she walked through the living room. I turned on the lamp that was on the table next to me.

"Sitting alone in the dark?" she asked.

"Yes," I said. I wasn't sure what the hell I was going to say to her. I was afraid. I was scared shitless is the reality of it. I had fallen for the woman in a mere month's time. *It was insane!*

"Well, that's pretty sad, Aiden," she said then turned away from me. "Good night."

I sat there, unsure of what to do. I watched Skye leave the

room and heard her treading up the stairs. After a few minutes, I got up and went up the stairs. Stopping at my bedroom door, I hesitated only a moment then I went inside. I knew what I needed to do to make things right.

10

CHAPTER TEN

Skye

I'd fallen asleep quickly. I was utterly exhausted. Looking up an old friend, I hung out with her until I had to come home. I didn't tell her everything. Just about the job and how much I loved being Joy's nanny. It wasn't a thing I'd ever even thought of being, and I was pretty proud of the positive changes I'd made in the kid's life. Joy had made changes in me too.

I had to admit to myself that I had no regrets. Not one. Getting involved with Aiden had taught me a lot. I couldn't regret him. But my heart hurt as I knew I couldn't allow myself to be used by him any longer.

I was worth more than that.

That night I was woken up by a soft kiss on the top of my head. "Hey," came his soft voice.

Turning over, I rubbed my eyes. "Aiden, don't." He'd never come to my bedroom before. I'd always gone to his. I had no idea what it meant that he was there, sitting on the edge of my bed the way he was.

I felt him take my left hand and he slid something onto my ring finger. "This belonged to my grandmother. I want you to have it, baby."

Though my eyes were blurry, I could see the shiny gold ring he'd put on my finger. "And what does this mean?"

"It means I want you, Skye Fox. I want everyone to know that you and I are a couple. I don't want to hide it any longer." He scooped me out of bed.

As I wrapped my arms around his neck, I asked, "Where are you taking me?"

"I'm taking you to our bedroom. I'll be moving your things into it in the morning before I start writing. And you and I will tell Joy, together. I think you're right about her being more than okay with this."

"I've thought about something else, Aiden. If we're going to make this official, then I can't take a salary for watching Joy anymore."

"You don't have to. What's mine is yours, baby. You won't be limited to that salary. I'll get you a card, so you'll have access to our money."

"Our money?" I asked him. "Aiden, that's your money."

He shook his head as he took me into the bedroom I was to think of as ours now. "Skye, if it hadn't been for finding you and all you brought to my world then I'd never have written again. I'm getting an enormous advance from my publisher for the novel you inspired. And, as you'll keep inspiring me, I think it's fitting that you have access to that money too."

"I still want to be a nurse someday," I said as he laid me down on the bed.

"And you will. As a matter of fact, I think you should use some of our money to get into a real nursing program. Why go the slow route when you can take the fast one?" He kissed me then. A sweet kiss that made my heart pound and melt all at the same time. When his lips left mine, he cupped my face in his hands. "I love you, Skye. I was foolish when I told you I wanted things to stay the way they were. The truth is, I was scared."

"Of me?" I asked, as the thought seemed ludicrous.

"I'm a man who writes about the scariest things. I was afraid of how society would look at me and how my daughter would see me. But nothing I can imagine is as scary as you leaving me. When you drove away today, I felt worse than I've ever felt, and I've had some bad times, baby."

Guilt flowed through me. "Aiden, I'm sorry. I didn't think …" His lips stopped me as he gave me another long kiss.

"You were right to do that. You were right to stand up for yourself. It was wrong of me to even ask that of you. After I had put Joy to bed, I started thinking. I thought about her being in your position, and I knew right then and there that I'd want to kick a guy's ass if he asked that of her. So, I went to the box at the top of my closet where my grandmother's wedding ring was and took it out. I vowed that if you came home, then I'd put that ring on your finger and let you know you're one of the two most important people in this world to me."

His words had a lump in my throat. All I could do was nod and kiss him again. My life was complete at that moment. I had a little family at the tender age of twenty-two, and I was overjoyed with that fact.

The End.

ABOUT THE AUTHOR

Mrs. Love writes about smart, sexy women and the hot alpha billionaires who love them. She has found her own happily ever after with her dream husband and adorable 6 and 2 year old kids.
Currently, Michelle is hard at work on the next book in the series, and trying to stay off the Internet.
"Thank you for supporting an indie author. Anything you can do, whether it be writing a review, or even simply telling a fellow reader that you enjoyed this. Thanks

©Copyright 2021 by Michelle Love - All rights Reserved

In no way is it legal to reproduce, duplicate, or transmit any part of this document in either electronic means or in printed format. Recording of this publication is strictly prohibited and any storage of this document is not allowed unless with written permission from the publisher. All rights are reserved.

Respective authors own all copyrights not held by the publisher.

❦ Created with Vellum

www.ingramcontent.com/pod-product-compliance
Lightning Source LLC
LaVergne TN
LVHW021736060526
838200LV00052B/3314